NEW NEIGHBORS

I walked toward Marlene's house, deliberately looking down at the sidewalk as I passed it. I didn't want anyone who happened to be looking out a window to think I was at all interested in the people who had moved in.

I strode briskly past Marlene's front lawn and didn't raise my eyes until I got to the maple tree.

"Oh!" I gasped, and came to an abrupt halt in front of the tree.

Something was hanging from it.

"Howww do you do?" it said, in a voice that sounded like Dracula. . . .

Critics' Corner:

"An enjoyable, believable story that children will appreciate for its humor as well as its handling of adolescent reactions and over-reactions."

—*School Library Journal*

"Conford again successfully uses first-person narrative for this book about Dorrie, a middle grader. . . . Good fun with obvious appeal." —*A.L.A. Booklist*

"The book is appealingly full of school happenings, zippy repartee, and pre-adolescent witticisms."

—*Horn Book*

Other Recommendations: Bulletin of the Center for Children's Books, University of Chicago; National Council of Teachers of English.

About the Author and Illustrator:

ELLEN CONFORD lives in Massapequa, New York, with her husband, her son, and assorted pets. Miss Conford believes that "children enjoy two kinds of reading experiences. They like to read about things that could never possibly happen to them, and they like to read about the sorts of things that happen to them all the time. I write about the latter." Among the popular books that have established her as a funny and accurate writer for children are *Felicia the Critic; The Luck of Pokey Bloom; Dear Lovey Hart, I am Desperate;* and *The Alfred G. Graebner Memorial High School Handbook of Rules and Regulations: A Novel.*

CHARLES CARROLL grew up in Boston and attended the Vesper George School of Art and the Boston Museum School of Fine Arts. He is a graphic artist, and there is a permanent collection of his works at the Boston Public Library. Mr. Carroll also runs his own gallery in Gloucester, Massachusetts.

me and the
terrible two

by Ellen Conford

Illustrated by Charles Carroll

AN ARCHWAY PAPERBACK
POCKET BOOKS • NEW YORK

ME AND THE TERRIBLE TWO

POCKET BOOK edition published January, 1977

Published by
POCKET BOOKS, a division of Simon & Schuster, Inc.,
A GULF & WESTERN CORPORATION
1230 Avenue of the Americas, New York, N.Y. 10020.

Archway Paperback editions are distributed in the U.S.
by Simon & Schuster, Inc., 1230 Avenue of the Americas,
New York, N.Y. 10020, and in Canada by Simon &
Schuster of Canada, Ltd., Markham, Ontario, Canada.

ISBN: 0-671-29809-7.
Library of Congress Catalog Card Number: 73-18393.
Printed in the U.S.A.

2 3 8 7

To John Keller

one

Thursday, August 28, was the worst day of my entire life. And I've probably had more bad days in my life than anyone in the entire Western Hemisphere. Like the time Arnie Short poured orange soda over my head on a class trip and I had to walk all over Central Park with bees dive-bombing my hair because it smelled sweet.

And the time I had the chicken pox, and for ten days I itched and my mother said, "Don't scratch," fourteen times an hour, and tied white sox on my hands so I couldn't scratch and give myself scars. She says I couldn't possibly remember, since I was barely five at the time, but that was only six years ago, and when you've had sox tied on your hands for two weeks while your whole body felt like one giant mosquito bite, *you don't forget.*

But all the other bad times I've had just melt away like vanilla ice cream under hot fudge sauce when I think of Thursday, August 28.

That was the day my best friend, Marlene Dreyfus, moved to Australia.

Australia, for heaven's sake! Other people move to Baltimore or Detroit, or some place where, if you can't go and visit them, at least you can call them on the phone after eight when the rates are low, but not the Dreyfuses. No, they have to move to Australia, which is the other end of the world, and almost entirely populated by sheep, dingos, kangaroos and geysers. Or is that New Zealand?

In any case, Mr. Dreyfus was going to help start a branch of his company in Australia, and at 12:31 P.M. on Thursday, August 28, they left in a taxi for the airport.

I waved goodby from the front steps of my house until the taxi turned the corner and was gone. I felt my eyes fill up with tears, and angrily swiped at them with my knuckles. Marlene wasn't crying now, I reminded myself. Marlene was *excited* about going to Australia, where, she told me, it was now winter, practically. Or spring, practically—I forget which. Everything is upside down, there, or backwards.

2

I sat down on the step below Sherman, and tried to hug him to make myself feel better. But it's very hard to hug a dog who is lying down. There's nothing really to get hold of.

"Oh, Sherman," I sighed.

He raised his head and yawned. Then he got up and walked down the steps without giving me so much as a comforting nuzzle.

"Stupid dog," I sniffled.

I felt in the pocket of my shorts for the wallet Marlene had given me as a goodby present. It was still there. I didn't have anything to put in it, since I'd spent all my money buying Marlene a book about horses to take on the plane with her, but I took out the wallet anyway and looked at the color photograph of Shirley Jones that had come with it in the plastic photo holder.

What would I do without Marlene? There are some people who have so many best friends they practically go into a frenzy trying to decide who their *best* best friend is, but I am not one of them. Marlene and I did everything together, and when there was nothing to do, we did that together too. She slept over at my house, I slept over at her house. We used to have the same piano teacher, and our mothers discovered we were both lousy pianists at practically the same time. In the summer we went to the community pool together. In the winter we walked to school together every day.

Now I would do everything alone.

"You'll make other friends," my mother had said.

But not next door. Next door would always be Marlene's house, no matter who moved in. It was Marlene's house, Marlene's big old maple tree with the low-hanging branch that jutted out over the sidewalk. We used to chin ourselves on that branch, counting each other's tries in chinning contests.

Ringling Brothers' Barnum and Bailey Circus could move into Marlene's house and I would hate them all, even the glorious white horses—because *nothing* could take the place of the best friend I'd ever had.

The Dreyfuses had barely left the house when a moving van pulled up backwards into the driveway. They couldn't wait, could they? Like vultures, I thought savagely, eager for the desert rat to croak, so they could swoop down on the corpse.

Disgusted, I stalked into the house, letting the screen door slam behind me. Only it didn't, because it has one of those things on it that make it close softly and slowly—which is a shame, actually, since there are times in your life when the sound of a slammed door is really the only thing that will satisfy you. This was one of the times.

"Dorrie? Come and have lunch," my mother called out.

5

"I'm not hungry," I muttered, slumping into a kitchen chair.

"Well, you have to eat," my mother said reasonably, as if a good lunch would solve everything. "Why don't you just have a nice glass of iced tea and a bologna sandwich?"

The bologna was on thick slices of dark, dark pumpernickel bread.

"I'll try to force something down," I sighed.

"You do that," my mother nodded.

"The moving van is next door already," I announced.

"I know. I heard it pull up. Did you see the people yet?"

"No. Who wants to see them anyhow? Marlene said there are two boys."

"Well, you just might," my mother said, "find out that they're very nice people."

"What difference would that make?" I asked irritably. "They can't replace Marlene."

"No, dear, they can't. But they could be your friends—if you'd let them."

I poked aimlessly at the crusts of bread left on my plate. My mother just didn't understand how I felt, and I was too miserable to argue. She couldn't see that you can't just replace a best friend like you can change a flat tire. How could she know how I'd feel, seeing those two boys take over Marlene's house, Marlene's tree, Marlene's yard—seeing them everywhere that Marlene ought to be, but wasn't any more?

I went up to my room and peered out my window. A car had joined the moving van, and the door of the house was wide open. Two men were carrying in an old, upright piano. A woman was standing on the lawn, watching them as if she were afraid they would chop up the piano and use it for firewood.

I noticed that the sky was becoming thick with gray clouds. I hope it rains, I thought, feeling nasty. All over your furniture.

That isn't very nice, I told myself sternly. No, it isn't, I agreed. With Marlene gone, I might as well get used to talking to myself. I would probably be doing it quite a lot from now on.

It wasn't much fun.

I turned back to the window. It had started to rain. But the doors of the moving van were being slammed shut. They'd finished just in time.

They certainly couldn't have had much furniture, I brooded. Then I remembered that the Dreyfuses had left a lot of their stuff because it was easier than shipping it to Australia, so the new people had probably just brought along the stuff they were very attached to, like that mangy piano, and their two kids.

I picked up my guitar and started strumming it. I can only play a little bit. Actually, I can only play a G chord. My father sometimes gets very upset when I try to strum anything else, because he says it sounds like a funeral march no matter how I play it, and would-I-for-God's-sake-learn-to-play-that-thing,-he'd-be-delighted-to-pay-for-the-lessons.

But, when there's nothing else to do, strumming on my guitar can be very soothing. To me, at least, if not to my father.

So I strummed, and sang along a little. I sang "This Land Is Your Land" and "Michael, Row Your Boat Ashore." Since I don't know how to play either of them, they both sounded pretty much the same. (Like a funeral march, actually.) But every once in a while, a note I sang happened to come out right with a chord I strummed, so I thought it sounded pretty good. But then, my old piano teacher said I had no ear for music whatsoever, so I could be wrong.

After a while, it stopped raining, and I stopped playing. I decided to take Sherman for a walk.

I trudged downstairs and got Sherman's leash. "Come on, Sherman!" I called, trying to make my voice sound enthusiastic, "Let's go out!"

Sherman stayed under the kitchen table, snoring softly.

"Come on, boy! Walk!"

"Dorrie," my mother pointed out, "he's asleep. He doesn't want to go for a walk."

"Well, I do." I crawled under the table to snap his leash onto his collar. "How come we never want to go for walks at the same time?"

Sherman woke up and gazed reproachfully at me through his shaggy mop of hair. At the moment, only one eye peered out through the mop, which is one more eye than he usually shows.

"Come on, boy!" I urged. I crawled back out from under the table and tugged on the leash a little. "Nice walk!"

Sherman yawned so wide I thought his mouth would crack.

"You're overdoing it," I told him. "It won't work."

He groaned, and snaked out from under the table reluctantly. He promptly sat down and held out his paw.

"How do you do?" I said, shaking it. He'll hold it there for a month if you don't shake it.

"Now, let's go." I tugged the leash and he heaved himself up as if he were eighty years old and had arthritis. Lassie could take acting lessons from Sherman.

Once we got outside though, he perked up. He realized by then that it was no use trying to con me, and besides, it had just rained, and while he's not too crazy about the rain, he loves to walk in the puddles. And drink them.

I walked toward Marlene's house, deliberately

looking down at the sidewalk as I passed it. I didn't want anyone who happened to be looking out a window to think I was at all interested in the people who had moved in.

I strode briskly past Marlene's front lawn and didn't raise my eyes until I got to the maple tree.

"Oh!" I gasped, and came to an abrupt halt in front of the tree.

Something was hanging from it.

two

 "Howww do you do?" it said, in a voice that sounded like Dracula.

Sherman sat down and held out his paw.

The boy, who was hanging upside down from the tree branch by his knees, reached his arm toward Sherman, but he couldn't stretch far enough. He folded his arms across his chest, and swayed gently back and forth.

"Are you our new neighbor?" the boy asked, still sounding like something out of a vampire movie.

"Actually," I said, "you're *our* new neighbor."

"Let us not quibble over unimportant tings," he intoned. "Vat is your blood type?"

11

Oh, brother, I thought, staring at this weird kid hanging from Marlene's tree like a bat.

"Why do you want to know?" I asked.

"I'm varry fussy about vat I drrrink," he said haughtily.

"Well, see you around," I said. I yanked at Sherman's leash.

But Sherman still sat there with his paw upraised, waiting for the boy to shake.

"Stupid dog!" I muttered, bending down to grasp his paw. "How do you do," I whispered. "Now, *let's go.*"

"How do you do!" the boy repeated.

I tugged Sherman along; he insisted on sniffing around the base of the tree, and I stared back at this kid while trying to pull Sherman away.

"Yike!" I shrieked.

Around the other side of the tree, hanging upside down from another branch, with his arms folded across his chest, was a kid who looked exactly like the first one. Or, at least, they looked exactly alike upside-down.

"Howdy," he said solemnly. "You the new school-marm?"

He sounded like John Wayne.

"What?" In total confusion now, I looked from one to the other, then back again.

"Are you his brother?" I asked the one who was talking like a cowboy movie.

12

"No," the other one answered, in what I guess was his normal voice. "Actually, I'm his father. I'm just very short."

"And I'm tall for my age," the second one said.

By now I was totally flustered. How did you talk to crazy people?

"What's your name?" the second one asked. It was the first normal thing either one of them had said.

"Dorrie Kimball."

"My name's Conrad," he said. "He's Haskell."

Haskell? Were they fooling around again, or was Haskell his real name? I decided it was better not to take a chance on making fun of his name, because sometimes parents name their kids very strange things.

"Well, hello," I said.

"Hello," said Haskell.

"Well . . . so long," I said stupidly. My neck was getting tired from craning it to look at them in the tree, and I was sick of the whole conversation—if you could call it a conversation.

"Aw, do you have to leave so soon?" asked Conrad. "You just got here."

"I'm not really his father," Haskell confided. "Our father divorced us."

This seemed to make Conrad furious.

"He didn't divorce *us*, you moron! He divorced our mother!"

13

"Same thing," Haskell said indifferently.

"No it's not," I said. "You shouldn't feel that way. I'm sure your father loves you very—"

"What do you know about it?" Haskell demanded.

"Well, nothing, I guess. But just because your father didn't get along with your mother, it doesn't mean—"

"It's none of your business!" Conrad yelled.

"All right, all right! I'm sorry," I said irritably. "I only meant—"

"Oh, go home," Haskell muttered.

"I thought you wanted me to stay," I said coldly. "I was just trying to be polite. I'll be delighted to go home." I pulled Sherman away from the tree, and turned back toward my own house.

Try to say something nice to people, I grumbled. See what happens. Kid shouldn't think his father doesn't love him, I told myself. I was just trying to make him *feel* better, and look at the thanks I get. "Go home!" Sure, I'll go home. And I wish you'd go back wherever you came from too.

I was still grumbling and muttering under my breath when I walked in the front door.

"What are you mumbling about?" my mother asked. "And wipe your feet."

"They're nuts."

"Who's nuts?"

"The new people. Stark, raving nuts. Better lock the doors at night."

I thought of the one who talked like Dracula. Who knows what *he* did after dark?

"For heaven's sake, Dorrie, you're always making snap judgments about people! You didn't even give them half a chance. I'm sure they're really very nice."

"I certainly did give them half a chance. I gave them *three-quarters* of a chance! You weren't even there, and you're telling me they're very nice."

"Oh, Dorrie," she sighed, "if only you'd make an effort to be friendly . . ."

I did make an effort, I thought darkly. And I got told to mind my own business. If they want to be friendly, let *them* make the effort from now on.

The next morning I awakened to the sound of loud, off-key singing and the pounding of rhythmic hammers.

"Ach du leiber augustine, septemberstine, octoberstine, ach du leiber augustine, ya da da da!"

Bang, bang bang bang BANG BANG BANG, bang bang bang, BANG BANG BANG—

I raced to my window. Next door, the two of them were kneeling on the ground in their yard, hammering something. The singing continued. Horribly. They couldn't carry a tune at all. You

15

didn't have to have an ear for music to realize that their singing sounded like the shrill screams of rampaging elephants.

I nearly collided with my father and mother at the top of the stairs.

"That is the most hideous cacophony I have ever heard," my father snarled.

My mother made soothing noises.

"Our new neighbors," I informed him. "The Weirdo Brothers."

"Don't they know it's barely the crack of dawn?" he demanded.

"Now, Hal, it's after nine," my mother said.

"Some people are still sleeping," he grumbled.

"Not any more they're not," I pointed out.

"Most people are already at work," my mother went on. "It's not as if it were Sunday."

"I am not at work," he said. "And there is no excuse for that ungodly racket at this hour."

My father is the editor and publisher of the *Brockton Center Leader,* which is the local newspaper and comes out once a week. It's true that most of the people on our block commute to the city to work, so we were probably the only ones who were still asleep at nine o'clock on a Friday morning. We *liked* to sleep late.

Now, it seemed, Haskell and Conrad were going to put an end to that.

After breakfast, my father decided he might as

well go to the *Leader* office, since he was up any-way. I went to my room to write a letter to Marlene.

"Dear Marlene,

"Although you only left yesterday, I—"

"Ach du leiber augustine, septemberstine, octo-berstine ..."

Weren't they ever going to stop? I slammed my window shut and went back to my letter.

"—I figured this letter will take longer to get to Australia than you will, so I'm writing right away. I miss—"

BANG BANG BANG BANG!

"—you already, but I hope you like Australia. The new people moved in practically before you—"

"Ach du leiber augustine, septemberstine, octo-berstine ..."

I clenched my teeth. My fingers clamped around the pen till I thought either the pen or my fingers would break.

"—moved out and they are really creeps. I know it's not your fault that your parents had to sell the house, but these two are mental cases. They are named Haskell and—"

"CONRAD YOU DOPE! You nailed that on backwards!"

Arrgghh! My pen dug so hard into the paper that it ripped a hole in it. I threw the pen across the room and savagely crumpled the letter; I hurled it in the general direction of the waste-basket and missed.

I stomped out of my room and downstairs.

"This town," I said menacingly, "ain't big enough for the three of us!"

My mother just grinned.

"You sound like John Wayne," she observed.

No, I realized with a shock.

I sounded like Haskell.

three

 The last few days before school my feelings were all muddled.

First I couldn't wait for school to start. Then I wished that summer would never end. Then I wished that Labor Day would hurry up and be over already. Then Labor Day was over and school was *definitely* going to start almost instantly, and I wished it were next June, right now. And then I figured, since there was nothing else to do, school might as well start.

And it did.

The first day of school my father said he would drive me, since he had to meet his photographer there. They were going to do a picture story about the beginning of the new school year.

"Will you take my picture?" I asked. I never give up hope. I must have asked him that at least a million times over the past five years, whenever his paper covers a school event, or the opening of something that I attend, or when there's a rodeo or circus or something that he takes me to see.

"No," he said, for the million and one-th time. "That would be nepotism."

Nepotism, my father once told me, is when you do a favor for a relative. It seems to me that people do that all the time, but my mother says my father has higher standards than most people.

"Just once," I said irritably, *"just once* I'd like to see my picture in your paper."

"Do something newsworthy," he said, "and I'll put it there."

Which is what he always says. At the moment, I couldn't think of anything particularly newsworthy to do, so I picked up my looseleaf and said, "I'm ready."

"I hope Dan is there on time for once," my father said.

Dan is his photographer. Dan once missed the ribbon-cutting ceremony when my father was covering the opening of the new junior high school, and they had to tape the ribbon back together and fake the ceremony all over again so that my father could have a picture of it for the paper. My father never forgot it.

Why did he keep Dan as a photographer if he was so unreliable? I asked my father.

"He works cheap."

He also goes to college at night. He has to show his press card everywhere he goes to take pictures, because the police are always stopping him and asking to see his identification. That's because he doesn't look like a photographer. My mother says he looks like a mugger.

"I hope Mrs. O'Neill turns out better than you expect," my mother said cheerfully.

"She won't."

"Well, you never can tell," she said.

Which is ridiculous, because of *course* you can tell. If everyone says "ugh" when you say "O'Neill" you get a pretty good idea of how popular she is. But my mother tends to look on the bright side of everything I'm not looking forward to, like a fluoride treatment at the dentist or a crummy teacher. She only sees disaster coming when she doesn't want me to do something I enjoy, like riding my bike to the shopping center, or going to the beach alone.

My father dropped me off in front of school and went to look for Dan.

Although it was early, there were already plenty of people milling around the school yard. It's strange—everyone says they hate to see school start again, but the first day everyone gets there a half-hour early as if they couldn't wait for the doors to open.

I went over to the entrance near the fifth and sixth grade classrooms.

"Hi, Dorrie; welcome back to Sing Sing."

Margaret Cooper was sitting on the top step, with her best friends, Serena Blood and Jackie Benbow. Margaret hardly ever spoke to me last year, even though we were in the same class.

"Hi," I said, squeezing past three boys sprawled on the bottom two steps.

"Who's your teacher?" asked Margaret.

"Mrs. O'Neill."

"Ours too," Margaret said, wrinkling her nose. Nobody made room for me on the step, so I leaned against the iron railing, which was very uncomfortable.

"Been out on the boat this summer?" I asked. That's like asking Margaret if she breathes regularly. Her family has a forty-foot cabin cruiser which they named the *Princess Margaret*, which just goes to show you what her family thinks of her. I personally would be embarrassed if my parents had a boat and named it *Princess Dorrie,* but Margaret thinks it's perfectly okay.

"Oh, sure," she said. "We even went to Connecticut over Labor Day weekend, to my aunt's house. She lives on the Sound, so we docked right in back of her house."

"Heard anything from Marlene yet?" Serena asked.

"No. They only left last week." Thinking of Marlene suddenly made me feel sort of hollow in the stomach. Even though they were talking to me, Margaret, Serena and Jackie were together, like Marlene and I used to be, and I was the outsider.

They seemed like the Three Bears, or something, sitting in a row on the step, and there I was, standing against the railing like I was getting ready to bust into their house and eat up their porridge.

I had this awful, left-out feeling, and if the teachers hadn't opened the doors to let us in just then, I actually might have started crying.

We went down the hall to our room.

Some teachers place the desks in a big horse-shoe, with the teacher's desk in front; some arrange them in clusters of three or four in different areas all over the room. That's the way we had them last year. Mrs. O'Neill's room had regular up-and-down rows, and as we came in and scrambled for places, she stood behind her desk with her arms folded and her lips in a narrow, tight line.

"Here's a seat, Dorrie," Margaret said, pointing to one in the row next to hers. Serena and Jackie were directly behind her. Surprised, I slid into it, even though I had been going to take another seat, so they wouldn't think I was trying to be pushy or anything.

"Hey, who's that?" Jackie asked, looking past me.

I turned around to look over at the next seat.

Oh no! Of all the rotten luck. One half of the dopey duet—either Haskell or Conrad, I didn't know which—was grinning broadly at me.

"Ve meet again," he said, leering like Dracula at the sight of a brand-new throat.

Jackie giggled.

"Where's your brother?" I asked.

"They stopped him at the border for carrying a phony passport."

"There's another one," I told Margaret, "just like this one. He must be in a different class."

"A brilliant deduction, my dear Watson!" he said, this time with an English accent.

"All right, class!" Mrs. O'Neill's voice cut through the babble like a saw. "We will now take attendance."

"Abbot, Charles."

"Here."

"Benbow, Jacqueline."

"Here."

"Berman, Wendy."

"Here."

"Blood, Serena."

"Here."

"Brady, Eileen."

"Here."

"Caplowitz, Mark."

"Here."

"Conger, Haskell."

"Present."

Mrs. O'Neill's head jerked up from the attendance sheet. Even her stony glare didn't stop the giggles immediately. She waited a moment, and then went on to finish the roll call.

Well, at least now I knew which one I had to put up with. Although it didn't make any difference, since they seemed to be carbon-copy creeps, but at least I'd know what to call him if I ever had the misfortune to have to talk to him.

Mrs. O'Neill took up most of the morning passing out books. The rest of the time she spent warning us to have them all covered by tomorrow. Which meant we had to lug five books home and back again, and four of them were big, heavy ones.

At lunchtime, Margaret surprised me again by saying, "Come on, Dorrie," so I followed her and Serena and Jackie to the lunchroom. Margaret had brought her lunch from home, so she said she'd save us seats while we got the hot lunch.

I bought my lunch and followed Serena and Jackie to the table where Margaret was sitting. As I was putting my tray on the table, somebody yelled, "Look out!"

The next thing I knew, something smashed into my back, and I went sprawling over the table propelling my lunch tray right into Margaret's chest.

"OHH, NO!" she wailed, jumping up and wiping frantically at the tomato juice and lime jello that dripped down the front of her white blouse.

Horrified, I didn't even stop to think about the stuff that was dripping down the front of *my* blouse. I whirled around to see who had knocked me over. There, with a stupid little grin on his face, stood Haskell.

"Sorry about that," he said weakly.

"You—you—" I sputtered. I clenched my fingers into tight fists.

"You can have my tomato juice if you want," he offered.

"I could kill you, Haskell," I said in a voice cold with fury.

"I'm Conrad," he corrected. And he ran.

I sank down onto the bench next to Jackie. Margaret and Serena had gotten a bunch of napkins and wet them at the fountain. They were trying to sponge off Margaret's blouse.

"Listen, I'm really sorry, Margaret," I said miserably. "I hope I didn't ruin your blouse."

"It's not your fault," she said. "Anyway, I have another one just like it. It's just that I feel so ooky and wet—I must look awful."

I looked at Margaret for a moment. She didn't look awful—Margaret never looked awful—but she did look pretty wet.

"Hey, why don't you stand in front of one of those blowers in the bathroom?" I suggested. "They dry your hands in a minute, I'll bet if you squat down a little and get right next to it it'll dry your blouse off."

"That's a good idea!" Margaret exclaimed. "I'm

going right now. I'll be back as soon as I'm dry. Save my seat."

My hamburger roll was partly soaked in tomato juice, so I picked the hamburger out of it and ate it plain. It really didn't taste very good that way.

"Are they twins?" Jackie asked me. "They look exactly alike."

"I guess so. Twin maniacs."

"I think they're sort of cute," Jackie said softly.

"Cute?" I shrieked.

"Well, yes. Sort of."

"Trade houses with me," I offered. "You won't think they're so cute."

"Jackie's going through a *phase*," Serena said sarcastically. "She thinks *Walter* is cute."

Walter is the school's head custodian. He is six foot six and walks like a gorilla. He has a tattoo of a snake on his bicep, and sometimes, when the boys ask him to, he flexes his bicep and makes the snake wriggle.

"I never said Walter is cute!" Jackie said hotly. "I said his *tattoo* is cute."

After a while, Margaret came back. "That really worked," she said happily. "And I don't think it'll leave a stain."

She was being pretty nice about it, considering that there were pink blotches all over the front of her blouse, but at least they were pale pink, and dry now.

"You've got some on you too, Dorrie," she said, pointing to my chest. "Maybe you'd better wash it off."

I looked down. It wasn't too bad, but it had all dried, and I didn't know if my mother would be able to get the stains out. *I* didn't have another blouse exactly like this one, but I wasn't so crazy about this one anyhow.

"Madam, your lunch."

Conrad was bowing low next to me and holding out a tray with a whole new meal on it.

"Wha—"

"Go ahead, it's for you."

"But I don't want another lunch!"

"I had the chef make it up especially for you," he went on, ignoring my protests. He set it down on the table in front of me.

"Hamburgair à la Horse," he crooned, in a French accent, "tomahto juice, and cole slaw wiz just a pinch of mothball extract."

Jackie giggled.

"Oh, oui, and ze specialty of ze house, green Jello."

"I don't want another lunch!" I said furiously. "Conrad, if you don't—"

"No, no, I'm Haskell. Conrad sent me. Gotcha!"

Serena and Margaret dissolved in laughter as he strolled off. Jackie turned to look after him.

"He's funny!" Margaret said.

"Yeah, funny like a plane crash," I said sourly.

"Which one was he?" Serena asked, confused. "Was he Haskell?"

"He said he was Haskell," Jackie pointed out.

"Well, he could have been kidding. I guess they do that a lot," Margaret said.

"Oh, yeah," I nodded. "They're a barrel of laughs."

"Why do you hate them so much?" asked Margaret curiously. "It was an accident, and no one else would have bought you a whole new lunch— I thought that was kind of nice."

I sighed, and shrugged my shoulders. There are some things people just have to find out for themselves.

four

On Saturday morning there were two letters for me. One was from Marlene. It was short, only two pages. She said she was busy getting settled, and very tired. Australia was okay, but she missed America. And me.

The other envelope was much smaller. I looked at it curiously before I opened it.

"Hey, I'm invited to a pajama party!"

"Whose party is it?" asked my mother.

"Margaret Cooper." I turned the invitation over and over, unbelievingly. "I wonder why she invited *me*."

"Maybe she likes you," my father suggested.

I was still trying to figure out why she'd invited me when my mother asked me to walk the dog.

"Oh, he doesn't have to go out," I said absently, as Sherman ran back and forth from the front door to the kitchen where we were sitting.

"Dorrie, he's practically hysterical," my mother said. "Don't tell me he doesn't have to go out."

"Oh, for heaven's sake," I grumbled. I tossed the invitation down on the table and stomped to the front door. Sherman whined urgently as I snapped on his leash.

Now, Sherman is a pretty big dog. A lot of Sherman is hair; piles and piles of fluffy white and gray hair. But under the hair there is also a great deal of dog. As my father says, Sherman walks *you,* rather than the other way around.

When I opened the door to go out, Sherman practically dragged me down the front steps. I couldn't even close the door—it was all I could do to hang on to the leash and follow him without falling down the steps and breaking my neck.

"Heel, Sherman, heel!" Half the time Sherman suffers from amnesia and completely forgets the meaning of the word "heel." It's like saying, "Slow down, ocean, slow down," as the waves engulf you, because the ocean is about as obedient as Sherman.

I wrapped the leash around my wrist a little, and practically cut off all the blood circulating to my arm, because Sherman kept pulling wildly at his end.

"Listen Sherman!" I shouted as my hand went numb.

But Sherman didn't listen. He dragged me down the street, and now I saw the reason for his excitement.

Haskell and Conrad were in front of their house and they had something—I didn't know what—on the end of a thin red leather leash.

When they saw us running toward them (Sherman was running; I think I was just being towed behind him, without moving my feet at all, like a water skier) they yelled, "Keep him away! Hold him!"

"I can't!" I yelled back. "Hold yours!"

One of them scooped up the little animal from the sidewalk. It was beige and white and looked kind of like a fuzzy eggplant.

Sherman reached Haskell and Conrad. He lunged at the boy holding the animal and knocked him to the ground.

"Get that beast out of here!" he screamed. His pet clawed frantically at his shirt, trying to get away from Sherman's wildly sniffing nose.

I yanked the leash as hard as I could, pulling Sherman off the boy sprawled on the sidewalk.

He leaped up and ran into his house, clutching the little thing to his chest.

"That stupid dog of yours ruined everything! Haskell and I were just getting him to walk with .

the leash when you and that killer came along."

"Killer!" I said indignantly. "Sherman's no killer. He was just trying to make friends."

"Make friends! He was going to rip Little Caesar to pieces. He's a killer."

"He wouldn't rip anything to pieces," I retorted. "He's as gentle as a—a—"

"Then why is he named after a killer?" Conrad demanded.

"He's not named after a killer," I insisted. "He's named after a famous general."

"What do you think generals *do*, stupid?"

"Don't call me stupid! Look, I'm sorry that my

dog scared your Caesar, or whatever his name is—"

"Little Caesar, dummy. It's a famous movie."

"Well, it can't be that famous, because I've never heard of it."

"That's because you're stupid!" he yelled.

Haskell came out of his house.

"He's just sitting there in his cage," he reported worriedly. "All scrunched up in a corner. He won't move."

"I'm sorry," I repeated. He looked so anxious about Little Caesar that I began to feel very guilty about the whole thing.

"Sherman didn't mean to scare your—whatever it is—"

"A guinea pig," Haskell said absently.

A guinea pig on a leash? Even for Haskell and Conrad that seemed strange.

Sherman had calmed down now, and was lying at my feet on the sidewalk, placidly gnawing on a rock.

"See? He's a very nice dog, really. He was just trying to be friendly."

They looked down at him.

"He has the instincts of a trained killer," Conrad said decisively. He stalked off toward his house.

"That's ridiculous," I snapped. "You can't train

35

Sherman to heel, let alone kill. All he can do is shake hands."

"That's the trouble," said Haskell. "If you'd trained him like any civilized dog, he wouldn't go around attacking defenseless animals."

"I'm sure Little Caesar will get over it," I said. "He probably just needs to be left alone a while so he can calm down a little."

"I don't know," Haskell said, shaking his head. "He looked pretty bad."

For that matter, so did Haskell.

He turned to walk away, then called back over his shoulder, "If I were you, I'd keep that dog inside."

"That sounds like a threat," I said, beginning to get angry again.

"Just a suggestion," Haskell said. But it didn't sound like a suggestion. It sounded like a threat.

My mother was standing at the front door.

"What was that all about?" she asked as I unsnapped Sherman's leash.

"Sherman scared their guinea pig," I said irritably. "They were teaching it to walk on a leash."

"A guinea pig on a leash?" my father said. "That's impossible."

"I don't know about that," I said disgustedly. "He probably heels better than Sherman already."

For dinner we had Mystery Pot Pie. Mystery Pot Pie is every leftover thing we had all week, thrown into a casserole with a can of beef gravy and some red wine, with a biscuit crust on top. Sometimes it turns out great, sometimes it turns out rotten. Depends on whether or not we had fish during the week.

This time it turned out especially good because there were some cut-up sausages in it, and my mother didn't try to sneak in any stringbeans or peas, like she usually does.

I was just reaching for some more when the doorbell rang.

It was Haskell. Or Conrad. Anyway, he handed me an envelope.

"What's this?" For one wild moment, I thought it was another invitation to something. I should have known better.

"The medical bill. For Little Caesar."

"What?"

"He had to go to the vet, and the vet gave him a sedative and put him on tranquilizers."

I opened the envelope. There was a piece of paper from a prescription pad. On it was written, "For Little Caesar—Office Visit and Medication —$7.00."

"He may need to go to a psychiatrist," he said. "If he does, we'll send you the bill for that, too."

"That's the dumbest thing I ever heard!"

"We may also sue you for damages. Little Caesar may be scarred for life."

"That's ridiculous. Sherman didn't lay a paw on him."

"Mentally scarred," he said grimly.

"You're the only one around here who's mentally scarred, Haskell."

"I'm Conrad," he informed me coldly.

"I told you they were crazy," I reminded my mother, after telling them why we had been given a medical bill for a guinea pig.

"I think it's rather funny," my mother said lightly.

"Will *you* pay the seven dollars?" I demanded.

"Oh, they're just joking."

"I'm telling you, they're not joking. They're nuts. They don't think this is funny at all."

"Don't get so excited," my father said.

"I'm not excited!" I shouted. "It's just that we're living next door to a couple of raving maniacs and everyone insists they're just a couple of funny kids."

"Well," my father remarked mildly, "at least you're not excited."

I called Margaret after dinner to tell her I could come to her pajama party.

"Who else is going to be there?" I asked, hoping this would give me an idea as to why I was asked to come.

"Oh, everyone," she replied happily. "I invited all the girls in the class."

Oh.

five

"Would you please tell me why it's so important for you to have new pajamas?" my mother demanded.

"Because my old ones are crummy," I wailed. "I can't go to a pajama party and wear those ratty old flannel things."

"I bought those 'ratty old flannel things' two weeks ago," my mother pointed out.

"But they were for *sleeping*," I said desperately, "not for parties. Look, if I were going to a regular party, you'd buy me a new dress, wouldn't you?"

"I might," she conceded, *"if* you needed one."

"So why are you being so mean just because it's a pajama party? A party is a party."

41

She frowned. "When you put it that way, it almost sounds reasonable."

"It *is* reasonable," I said anxiously, beginning to detect that she was softening up. "And logical."

"All right, all right," she sighed. "We'll get you new pajamas."

"When?"

"This week. Before the party, don't worry."

"When this week?"

"I guess it had better be tomorrow, otherwise you'll nag me for the next three days."

"Oh, thank you, thank you!" I cried, flinging my arms around her and hugging her, hard.

"Dorrie!" she gasped. "My neck!"

I had managed to avoid Haskell and Conrad in school, which wasn't too hard, since they were avoiding me too. In class, Haskell had made friends with several of the boys already, and if I happened to pass him during the day, he just glared at me.

But Wednesday afternoon, Mrs. O'Neill changed everything.

"As you know," she began, "next month is Children's Book Week."

As who knows? I wondered. This was the first I'd heard about it.

"And I thought we'd do something special to

observe the occasion. Something the whole school would enjoy."

"Close school for the week," Warren Schultz whispered.

"SO," she went on loudly, ignoring the giggles, "we're going to form committees and each committee will prepare a project based on a famous book."

Well, that didn't sound so bad. In fact, it sounded kind of interesting.

And then Mrs. O'Neill assigned committees.

"Dorothy Kimball, Serena Blood, Charles Abbot, Haskell Conger."

NO! NO!

"Dorothy, you'll be the chairman."

Haskell leaned over toward the aisle and pretended he was having an appendicitis attack.

Me, on a committee with HIM? Me, chairman of HIM? How could I keep on avoiding Haskell if we were on the same committee? And if we couldn't avoid each other, wouldn't he do all he could to make me miserable? Of course he would. He hated me. He even hated my dog. He'd probably sabotage the whole project. Whatever it was going to be. Just to get even with me for Little Caesar's nervous breakdown.

"Now I'll give you a few minutes to get together with your committees," Mrs. O'Neill said, "and start your preliminary discussions. You'll probably need some meetings after school to work on this, but we will set aside a period each day for committee conferences."

After school, I thought darkly. That's when the trouble will come.

"Okay," I said, my voice sounding weak and unchairmanlike, "anybody got any ideas?"

My committee clustered around my chair. Out of the corner of my eye I looked at Haskell. He perched on my desk, staring at me expectantly. He didn't say a word, just sat and stared, as if he couldn't bear to miss a thing. I was sure he was deliberately trying to make me nervous. It worked.

"We could do a diorama," Serena suggested. "A scene from a book."

"Oh, everyone's going to be doing that," Charles said scornfully. "We ought to do something different."

"Like what?" I asked.

"Well, I don't know," he shrugged. "We haven't had time to think up anything yet, really."

"Okay, well," I said nervously, glancing over at Haskell. He was still gazing intently at me. "How about we all think up some things tonight, and be ready with them tomorrow? Let's say we'll each think of three books and a project for each book. Then we can choose the best idea."

"Okay," Charles said.

"Well, I'll try," Serena promised uncertainly.

I looked at Haskell. His face was thoughtful, his forehead wrinkled with concentration.

"Don't rightly recollect whether I've read three books," he drawled, in his cowboy voice.

I knew it, I thought angrily. He's going to wreck the whole thing if he can. Just you try, Haskell. Just try it.

"Well, when you learn to read, Haskell, let us know."

"You kicking me off your committee, Oh Great Chairman?"

I wish I could, I thought fervently. I only wish I could. But to Haskell I said, "No. Just be prepared to contribute something to it."

"Yes, ma'am," he said humbly. "Yes, honorable chairman. I will, ma'am."

I was not looking forward to the next couple of weeks.

My mother picked me up at school to take me to buy pajamas.

"I'm on a committee with It," I said grimly, when she asked me how school was.

"It? Who's It?"

"You know, It. Haskell. One half of the Disgusting Duo."

"Oh, *that* It." She grinned.

"It's not funny, you know."

"I know."

45

"He's going to ruin everything."

"Look, you have to try and understand them, Dorrie. They've had a difficult time."

"So *I* have to suffer because they have it tough?"

"I got a letter from Annette Dreyfus today. She told me their parents are divorced; their father never comes to see them; he doesn't take any interest in them at all, apparently. They've really had their problems."

"So they make sure everyone else has problems too."

"Dorrie, they're not evil, for heaven's sake. They're very intelligent boys who've been left on their own a lot. That's all."

"Then maybe their mother ought to hire an armed guard to keep an eye on them."

"You're not even trying to understand, Dorrie," she said impatiently.

"Well neither are you!" I fumed.

She stopped trying to convince me that Haskell and Conrad were just a couple of hard-luck kids from a broken home, but even talking about them had an effect on our shopping trip. The discussion had put my mother and me in such a sour mood that we couldn't agree on anything for the rest of the afternoon.

Everything I liked my mother said I couldn't have. And for no good reason at all.

"But this is beautiful!" I said, fingering a white satin nightgown with a matching lace robe.

"Dorrie, that's a peignoir set. It's for brides."

"So what? I love it!"

"It doesn't come in children's sizes. It's not for children!"

"You could put a hem in it," I persisted.

"Don't be ridiculous," she snapped. "It would take more than a hem before that would fit you."

What she really meant was that she didn't want to spend forty-five dollars, which is what it cost. When I looked at the price tag, I realized it was hopeless. But if she'd just said so in the first place—

"How about this," she suggested, after she had led me away from the women's lingerie department and practically hurled me into the pre-teen section.

"Ugh," I said, making a face. Ski pajamas with a red sailor top and navy blue pants, which were ribbed at the ankles.

"I think they're cute," she said.

"I think they stink," I grumbled.

"What about this?" She showed me a pair of flannel pajamas with elastic at the wrists and ankles so that a little of the material formed gathered cuffs. There were little pink and blue roses all over it.

"For babies," I sneered.

Her mouth turned down and she set her lips tightly together.

"Keep this up, Dorrie, and I swear I'll buy you pajamas with feet and a button-down backside."

We finally compromised on a soft, fuzzy granny gown, with long sleeves and a frill of lace at the wrists and the neck. It was pretty; it had tiny yellow flowers on little green leaves all over it.

"Isn't it nice?" asked the saleswoman pleasantly. "All the girls seem to like this."

"It's all right," I mumbled.

My mother glared at me.

When we got home, Haskell and Conrad were riding their bikes in a big circle in the street in front of their house. They had their hands folded across their chests, and were singing "Ach du lieber augustine."

"They're going to kill themselves," my mother predicted, "riding like that."

"I hope so," I said passionately.

When she opened the front door, we spotted an envelope on the floor under the mail slot. "What's this?" she asked. "We already got our mail today."

She turned it over.

"It's addressed to Sherman!" she exclaimed.

I snatched it from her.

48

"They're at it again!" I ripped open the envelope. "I told you they were crazy!"

Inside was a piece of paper with words cut out of newspapers and magazines, pasted into a message. It said:

We ARE WatcHing You. Do not

think you wiLL get Away with it.

We have ouR MeTHOds OF reVenge.

"Well," my mother said uncertainly.

"You see?" I cried. "You see? They're dangerous!"

"Poor Sherman," she said absently, patting his shaggy head. "An anonymous letter."

"It's not funny!"

"I know it's not funny, Dorrie," she said. "Even though they probably meant it as a joke."

"They didn't!" I insisted.

"Whether they did or not, I'll call Mrs. Conger later and we'll talk it over. Now, don't let it worry you."

Don't let it worry me! My dog receives a threatening letter from a pair of homicidal maniacs, and I shouldn't let it worry me!

"A fine how do you do, isn't it, Sherman?" she said sympathetically.

Sherman held up his paw.

SIX

 My mother said Mrs. Conger was very nice. Young and pretty and very concerned about her juvenile delinquents. She also worked as a research chemist, and therefore didn't spend as much time as she'd have liked with Haskell and Conrad. But, of course, they needed the money and what could she do?

"It's very hard for her, Dorrie," my mother said.

"All right, all right," I said impatiently, "that's too bad and everything, but what about the note?"

"Oh, they admitted they wrote it. They're very honest, whatever else you might think of them."

"Great. So they're honest weirdos."

"They said they just wanted to scare Sherman because he scared their guinea pig."

"Oh, yeah, that makes a lot of sense."

"Well, of course they felt they were using Sherman to get even with you. I don't say it makes sense, I just—"

"Revenge. My dog for their guinea pig."

"I guess that was the idea. But they said they never meant to do anything else. The note itself was all."

"And you still say they're not psycho?" I demanded.

"I *hate* the way you toss that word around, Dorrie," she said irritably. "Of course they're not psychotic. They're just—"

"Nuts," I declared.

The note kept bothering me. My mother seemed reassured by her talk with Mrs. Conger, but I wasn't at all convinced that Haskell and Conrad had no further plans for revenge on Sherman. My mother had given the note to Mrs. Conger, and she'd ripped it up after talking to her sons, but I could still see it as I closed my eyes that night and tried to sleep.

"Don't let it bother you," my mother had said. But I couldn't help it. I was too angry and upset to think of anything else.

Your project, I reminded myself. You have to

have three ideas by tomorrow. How will it look if *you* don't come up with some suggestions for the committee?

Alice in Wonderland . . .

But I couldn't concentrate on white rabbits and grinning cats. All I could think about were threatening words clipped out of newspapers, then carefully, hatefully pasted on a piece of stationery. . . .

I woke up the next morning with the most fantastic idea for our project. I couldn't imagine where I'd gotten it—I hadn't been able to think of anything before I fell asleep. It just came to me, out of no place, as I was getting out of bed.

"Dad," I began, after he had had two cups of coffee. "We have to do a project for Children's Book Week. Now I have this terrific idea for my committee—did you know I'm the chairman?"

"Your mother told me."

"Oh, well, see the thing is, I need some help."

"What do I have to build?" he asked suspiciously.

"No, nothing like that. Anybody could do *that*."

"Uh oh. I smell something big and expensive coming up."

"Well," I said meekly, "I don't know how expensive it would be, but it is kind of big."

"You'd better stop trying to break it to me gently. What is it?"

"A newspaper," I said eagerly. "I want to know if you could print us up a newspaper."

"A newspaper! But that's a very big—"

"Well," I said defensively, "I told you it might be big."

"But, Dorrie, *you're* supposed to be doing the project."

"We will! We'll do all the writing and the pictures and everything. All you have to do is print it. Would that be very expensive?"

"All I have to do is print it," he repeated, shaking his head. "You'd better tell me more."

So I did. I told him all my ideas, and while he listened, he began to smile. I could see that he thought it was a good project. My mother was nodding and grinning too.

"I think that's the cleverest thing," she said admiringly. "Don't you think so, Hal?" She was now on my side, I noted triumphantly. Half the battle was won!

"And you know," she went on, "the day after the *Leader* comes out, the printers have practically nothing to do. They're there all day anyway, with no work, so the labor wouldn't amount to anything at all. You'd just have to provide the paper."

"Unless there's an outside job to be run off," my father pointed out.

But I could see he was coming around.

"You're sure it will be only four pages—"

"Oh, sure," I said excitedly. "Only four pages."

"Well, I guess I could—"

"Oh, thank you! Thank you!" I yelled. I flung my arms around him just as he put down his coffee cup.

"DORRIE!" he howled. His cup overturned and coffee splashed all over the table and dribbled down into his lap.

"I'm sorry," I said feebly, backing out of the way as he leaped up from his chair. He glowered at me.

At lunch everyone wanted to talk to Margaret about her pajama party. The girls did, that is. The boys just snickered and made fun of the whole thing.

"Oh, Jackie," said Warren Schultz to Haskell, "what bee-yoo-tee-full pajamas!"

"Oh, Margaret," said Haskell to Warren in a high, squeaky voice, "you silly thing. This is my scuba diving outfit."

For some weird reason, all the boys thought that was absolutely hilarious. Jackie giggled too, because they used her name. But, as Serena pointed out, Jackie didn't care what the boys said about her, as long as they noticed her.

"Do you have fifteen beds in your house?" asked Mark Caplowitz from the next table.

"Of course not!" Margaret replied.

"Well, where are fifteen people going to sleep, then?" he demanded.

"Sleep!" Margaret laughed. "A pajama party isn't for sleeping."

"Then why do you wear pajamas?" he persisted.

"Because it's a pajama party. At night."

"Stupid," Mark muttered, shaking his head. "Stupid."

"Oh, you're just jealous," Jackie said, wiggling her fingers at Mark. "I'll bet you wish you could come."

"Are you crazy?" Mark squealed. He looked around wildly, as if he were afraid someone had heard. He turned back to his own table and hunched over his sandwich.

"Are we going to stay up all night?" asked Eileen Brady. She had stopped to talk to Margaret on her way to the garbage cans.

"Sure," said Margaret. "That's the whole idea."

"Oh, boy," gloated Eileen. "My mother would never let me stay up all night at *home*."

"Well, this is special," said Margaret grandly.

Although Margaret had been pretty nice during the few days we'd been eating lunch together, I could see that—just like last year—she wanted to be in charge of things. Her party made her important, and giving the party put her in charge of things for the whole week, practically, since all the girls talked about was the pajama party. Margaret was the center of attention, and you could see that she thought that was just the way it should be.

"Listen, Serena," I began, eager to tell her about the newspaper. "I had the greatest idea for our project this morning—"

"Oh, we can talk about that later," Serena interrupted. "Listen, Margaret, should we bring blankets or anything?"

"Oh, yes, I meant to tell you . . ."

Annoyed, I turned back to my lunch. This afternoon, when we had committee meetings, *I'd* be in charge. Serena would *have* to listen to me then.

"Okay, is everybody ready with their ideas?" I asked. I tried to make myself sound like I really wanted to hear what my committee had thought up, but actually I couldn't wait for them to finish telling their ideas so I could get to mine.

Charles handed me a piece of paper. I read his three sentences out loud.

"One: Make a scale model of Robinson Crusoe's desert island.

"Two: Make a model of H. G. Wells' Time Machine.

"Three: Make a map showing Phileas Fogg's route in *Around the World in Eighty Days.*"

"Those are good ideas," I said briskly. "What about you, Serena?"

"Well," she began hesitantly, "I could only think of two. Maybe we could do a play—I mean, one scene, you know, from a book. I thought since there were four of us we might do *Little Women.*"

"Little Women!" Charles sneered. "You don't expect us to dress up like girls, do you?"

"Uh, no, Serena," I said gently. "I don't think that would work out too well for us."

Haskell was laughing at me. Not out loud, but inside, I knew he was laughing hysterically.

"Well then, the only other thing I could think of was to do a poster. You said you didn't want to do any dioramas."

"What kind of a poster?"

"Oh, you know, like the cover of a book."

Charles made a face. "You didn't work very hard on those ideas, did you?" he asked disdainfully.

"Well, I couldn't think of anything else!"

Your turn, It, I thought to myself. Aloud I said, "Haskell?"

"I couldn't think of anything either," he said casually. "We had company last night and I was tied up."

He looked at me pointedly. The "company" had been my mother, of course.

"Too bad they untied you," I murmured. Charles laughed.

"All right," I said eagerly. "Here's my idea. I'll be very honest with you before I tell you what it is. I think it's a fantastic idea."

"How modest," Haskell simpered.

"At least," I said, "I *had* an idea."

"It must be awful lonely up there," Haskell said, poking a finger against my forehead. I had the distinct feeling he wanted to pull a trigger.

I swatted his finger away as if it were a mosquito.

"It's a newspaper. My father will print it up for us himself, and it'll look really professional. All we have to do is write the stories and draw some pictures."

"What kind of a newspaper?" Charles asked curiously.

"A special edition of the *Leader,* put out just for Book Week."

"Oh, no, you mean with book reports in it?"

"No, nothing like that," I said. "This will be putting famous books into news stories, with headlines and pictures and things. Like for instance, take *Alice in Wonderland.* The headline would say, 'Girl Falls Down Rabbit Hole. Alice Tells of Strange Adventures.' Then you could have a news article underneath it, and I thought it could end, 'She is now under psychiatric examination at the county hospital.' "

"That's not bad," Charles said thoughtfully. "But could we fill up a whole newspaper with that stuff?"

"Sure we could. It'll only be four pages, and we could do drawings and things if we run out of ideas."

"I think it's a *good* idea," said Serena. She sounded interested for the first time since we began the project.

"We might," said Haskell suddenly, "do classified ads too."

This was so unexpected that I was speechless.

"For instance," he went on with a little grin, "Lost, Flock of sheep. Owner heartbroken. Generous reward. Call Bo Peep."

"Or," Charles suggested, "Real Estate: Large house with 14 bedrooms desperately needed. Contact old woman in shoe."

"And we could have the Recipe of the Day," Serena broke in. "Blackbird pie. Take four and twenty blackbirds and a *very* big pie plate—"

I laughed, and so did Charles. "If she can think of something to write," he whispered, "this must be a good idea."

"Can anyone besides me type?" I asked. "We have to make neat copies for the printers."

"I can type," Charles volunteered. "But not fast."

"That's okay," I said, relieved. "We can divide up the typing between us."

"And I can do the pictures," offered Serena.

"Oh, listen," I remembered guiltily, "we didn't take a vote on this. Maybe we should—"

"I vote yes," Serena said.

"We don't have to vote," Charles said impatiently. "You know we're all for it."

"Haskell?" I looked over at him. I didn't mean for my voice to come out sounding like I was daring him to object, but it did. It was just that it made me nervous to have to talk to him, so I tried not to sound nervous, and ended up sounding like Mrs. O'Neill.

"You're the chairman," he shrugged. "Whatever you say."

"We want to choose something the whole committee agrees to," I said primly. "So we'll all want to work on it and make it good."

"Let's hear it for democracy," Haskell said scornfully.

I turned my back on him. I was sure he thought the idea was good, but didn't want to say so, because it was *my* idea.

Okay, be stubborn, Haskell, I said to myself. With you or without you, this committee is going to turn in the best project in the class.

seven

"Don't forget," Margaret reminded me on Friday, "to bring your blankets. If you have a sleeping bag, that's the best thing, really. That's what I'm going to use."

Well, it seemed to me that since it was Margaret's house, she could perfectly well use her own bed, but I suppose that she wanted to keep in the spirit of the thing. Now, if she'd had my mother, she'd have had to put up a fight. "What do you need a sleeping bag for?" would be the first question. "You have a perfectly good bed. And you said you weren't going to be sleeping anyway."

Which is almost exactly what my mother said when I told her I needed a sleeping bag.

"You don't need a sleeping bag," she said firmly.

"But I do! Everyone else has one."

"Margaret is not 'everyone else.' You can take a blanket."

"But I'll have to lie on the *floor*."

"You roll yourself up in the blanket. Or take two blankets. I went to plenty of slumber parties, and I never had a sleeping bag."

"They probably didn't have sleeping bags when you were young," I grumbled. "And besides, I—"

"Forget it, Dorrie!" she snapped. "And stop shoving that newspaper in my face."

There was a beautiful sleeping bag advertised in the afternoon paper, and it was on sale for $18.99. It had white stars on a navy blue background, and the lining was red and white stripes. I thought $18.99 was very reasonable, considering it was practically a portable bed.

So when my father came home I met him at the front door with the ad. My mother was in the kitchen and I thought this would be a good time to discuss the sleeping bag with him.

"Dorrie, could I hang up my jacket?" he asked patiently. He tried to work his way around me to get to the coat closet. Sherman was sitting against the closet door with his paw held up, and my father was having kind of a hard time.

"You can see I really need it," I finished anxiously, "and it's on sale. It's a *bargain*. What do you think? Can I get it?"

"Did you ask your mother if you could have it?"

"Well," I hesitated, trying to find the right words to explain it.

"What did she say?"

"I said NO!" my mother yelled from the kitchen.

She doesn't miss a thing.

"I wish you wouldn't try to get me to say yes to something when your mother has already told you no," he said reproachfully.

"I don't understand why not," I scowled. "You're supposed to take your complaint all the way to the president of the company if you can't get any satisfaction from anyone else. You said so yourself in your 'Consumer Facts' column."

"It's not the same thing," he said gently. "But it's nice to know that you read my paper."

I argued practically all evening, and got no place. They just couldn't understand why it was so important to have a sleeping bag, and the more they couldn't understand, the more urgently I wanted one. I kept telling them they didn't understand me, and they kept asking me to explain whatever it was they didn't understand about me, and of course, I couldn't.

Finally, my mother simply got up, went into the

bedroom and locked the door. She turned on the television good and loud, and didn't come out for the rest of the evening. My father, whom I turned to the moment she left the room, told me he had a lot of work to do. He went into his study and began to pound his typewriter. He was probably writing something like "wxyzplmbghtylop," because I know he was just typing fast to sound busy, and to drown out my voice.

So I went upstairs and slammed my own door, even though I couldn't lock it, which doesn't seem fair. I picked up my guitar and played "This Land Is Your Land" about twelve times, and sang it as loud as I could, until my throat was practically raw, but no one paid any attention. I'll bet they didn't even hear me.

Saturday morning at nine A.M.:

"ACH DU LIEBER AUGUSTINE SEPTEM-BERSTINE OCTOBERSTINE ACH DU LIE-BER AUGUSTINE YA DA DA DA!" Bang bang bang bang BANG BANG BANG!

"Oh no!" I howled. I was jolted out of a lovely dream in which Haskell, in a red, white and blue cement sleeping bag, had fallen into Tebbits' Lake.

"Not again!" I tore off my pajamas and threw on jeans and a shirt. I raced downstairs, grabbed a jacket out of the coat closet and charged out the back door.

"Ach du lieber augustine . . ."

I hurtled over the fence between our yards and faced a startled Haskell and Conrad. They stopped, hammers in midair, and stared at me.

"Some people," I announced furiously, "are still sleeping."

"Well, glad you're not one of them."

"I would be," I retorted, "if you would have the decency to do your hammering and screeching at a reasonable hour."

"Aww, did we wake you up? Well, we're right powerful sorry, aren't we, Conrad?"

"Right powerful," Conrad nodded. "Yessir."

"Listen, creep—"

"CREEP?" Haskell leaped up and swatted me lightly in the face with his fingers. "Poltroon! No one calls me creep and lives. I challenge you to ze duel!"

He sprang into a fencing position and held his hammer like a sword. "EN GARDE!"

"En garde yourself, you moron!" I snatched the hammer from him and flung it across the yard. "If you don't stop this insane racket every morning—"

A window opened in his house.

"What's all the noise?" asked Mrs. Conger.

"Just a neighborly visit," said Conrad.

"About the noise *they're* making," I added indignantly. Couldn't she hear the hammering? Couldn't she hear the singing, which sounded very much like two screaming pigs stuck in a mailbox?

"It is kind of early for that, boys," she said. "Why don't you leave it till a little later?"

She pulled her head back in and shut the window.

I nodded with grim satisfaction. It was the same feeling as when you're five years old and can stick out your tongue and say, "So there!"

I climbed back over the fence.

My father's head was just emerging from his window.

"Can't you keep it down?" he snarled at me. "Don't you know what time it is?"

The Congers' back door slammed violently shut.

I had to lug a crummy, brown army blanket to Margaret's and I carried my pajamas and stuff in a plastic shopping bag with "VOTE FOR MCCLENDON" on it. I didn't even have a pajama bag. I was sure no one else would have to bring their things in a shopping bag, and sleep in an itchy wool blanket which my father must have gotten from someone who'd fought in World War II.

But, actually, no one seemed to notice when I got to Margaret's house. A lot of the girls were there already, clustered around the fireplace in Margaret's family room. That was a big room right next to the kitchen, with dark wood walls and a soft, gold carpet. It wouldn't be too bad sleeping on that, I thought.

"Hi, Dorrie," Margaret greeted me. "We're popping corn. It'll be ready in a minute."

I'd never seen anyone actually pop corn in a fireplace, so I dropped my stuff on the floor and went over to watch. As a matter of fact, I thought, the only popcorn I ever saw came in a big cellophane bag, or in a wax cup at the movies. I couldn't wait to try authentic, old-fashioned fireplace popcorn.

Serena handed Margaret a big bowl and they dumped the popcorn into it, and poured melted butter from a little pot over it.

"Okay everybody, dig in!" The butter was nice, but a lot of the popcorn was burnt, and some of it hadn't popped. The stuff that *wasn't* burnt and *had* popped tasted practically like the popcorn that comes in the cellophane bag. Except not so salty. I munched, disappointed, and nearly broke my tooth on an unpopped *and* burnt kernel.

But everyone said it was delicious.

"I think it's nice to have something homemade for a change," said Margaret's mother, who'd been supervising the popping.

"Oh, homemade is always better than the store," Eileen Brady said, nodding her head vigorously.

Everyone was there by eight o'clock, and Margaret's mother was in the kitchen making little pizzas on English muffins for us when the phone rang.

"It's for you, Jackie," she called.

"Me?" Jackie hopped up. "Who is it?"

"I don't know," said Mrs. Cooper. "A boy."

Jackie dashed into the kitchen. We all got very quiet, and tried to hear what she was saying. Which was hardly anything. What she was doing mostly was giggling. As far as I could tell, the only words she spoke were hello and goodby.

She ran back into the family room and flung herself onto the floor, still giggling.

"Who was it?" demanded Margaret.

"I don't know," she giggled.

"What did he want?" asked Serena.

"He said, did I like his tattoo!" Jackie rolled herself into a ball on the floor.

"Was it WALTER?" gasped Eileen.

"No, just one of the boys." Jackie pulled her knees up to her chest and clasped her arms around them. She sighed. She looked very pleased with herself.

Margaret frowned. "I wonder who it was."

"Probably Warren," said Serena, making a face.

The phone rang again.

"Dorrie Kimball!" Margaret's mother called in.

"For me?" Maybe something's wrong at home, I thought anxiously. I ran to the kitchen and picked up the receiver.

"Hello?"

"Is this Dorothy Kimball?" asked a strangely familiar voice.

"Yes. Who's this? What is it?"

"This is the Albermarle Dance Studio, and if you can answer just one question, you will win ten free dance lessons with Mr. Smoot, our trained ape. Are you ready for your question?"

I didn't know whether to be angry, or to start giggling, like Jackie.

"Who is this?"

"All right," the caller said, "here is the question. For ten free dance lessons with Mr. Smoot, can you identify this mystery voice?"

"AIIYEEEE!" A screeching howl exploded in my ear. It was so loud and unexpected that I dropped the receiver.

I heard someone talking at the other end, but I left the receiver dangling from the cord, thunking against the wall.

Margaret's mother looked over at me. "Everything all right?"

I nodded.

"Are you finished?"

I nodded again. She watched me put the receiver back on the hook.

I wandered back to the party. Was it Haskell? It didn't sound like Haskell. But, I reminded myself, Haskell can sound pretty much like anyone he wants to.

"Dorrie? Who was it?"

"The Albermarle Dance Studio," I said, beginning to giggle myself now. I told them about the mystery voice.

"That was probably just a joke," Eileen said soberly.

"We *know* it was a joke, Eileen," Wendy Berman said.

"Let's get into our pajamas now," Margaret suggested abruptly. "Anyone who's shy can use the bathroom. It's right over there."

I pulled my nightgown out of my shopping bag. I'm not shy, I reassured myself. I yanked off my slacks and shirt and slipped the gown over my head, on top of my underwear. I did it so fast that I don't think anyone noticed. Then I saw that a lot of other girls were also putting their pajamas and nightgowns on over their underwear.

The phone rang again.

"Margaret, I will never get these pizzas made at this rate," her mother threatened.

"I'll get it," Margaret said. She hopped into the kitchen, trying to get one foot into her pajamas. They were red and black with a Chinese collar and gold clips down the front.

"It's for you again, Dorrie," she said.

Oh, no, I groaned inwardly. I'll bet it *is* Haskell, and he's going to ruin this party, and all because he hates me. You'd think it was enough to ruin my sleep, and ruin my committee, and ruin our block and—

"Hello?" I said warily.

"King Kong calling," said a deep voice. "Want to swing Saturday night?"

"Will you stop!" I yelled into the phone. "Don't call me again!"

"Does that mean you won't go out with me?" he asked, in a slow, sad voice.

I slammed down the phone.

This time I wasn't sure it *was* Haskell. Or Conrad. Of course, I couldn't really tell, but I didn't think even they could manage such a deep voice.

So when everyone pestered me to tell them what was going on, all I could say was I didn't know.

After we had the pizzas, Margaret's mother left us alone, and Margaret opened a big leather pouch and dumped a whole pile of stuff on the floor in front of her.

"Where did you get this?" Serena asked, amazed. She pawed through lipsticks and eye shadow brushes—a whole bunch of cosmetics.

"Oh, it's some stuff my mother doesn't want any more," Margaret said airily. "I thought it would be fun to try some of it."

Everyone scrambled to grab something, and for the next hour Margaret passed around a mirror, and people ran in and out of the bathroom to use the mirror in there, while we made ourselves up.

"What do you think of this?" Wendy asked the group, as she applied lipstick.

"Ooh, it's brown," grimaced Serena. "It looks awful."

"You think so?" Wendy asked uncertainly. She peered over Jackie's shoulder to look in the hand mirror. "I thought it looked nice. Do you think maybe it's supposed to be eye shadow?"

I was holding a metal thing which looked like a pair of scissors at one end, and wondering what I was supposed to do with it when Jackie said, "That's to curl your eyelashes. You put mascara on, and then you press your eyelashes in that and they look longer. Here, I'll show you how."

She did it to herself, then handed me the mascara wand. "Just put it on your top lashes. Use a lot, that makes them look real thick."

So I did. Then I tried to slip my eyelashes in between the rubber edges of the curler.

"Ouch!" I cried. "I think I caught a piece of my eyelid."

"Just do the tips of the lashes," Jackie advised. "Or you might pull them off."

The phone rang. I froze.

"It's for *you* again, Dorrie," Margaret said. She looked annoyed.

I put down the eyelash curler and hauled myself

up from the floor. I walked to the phone like the condemned man walks the last mile.

"Hello?"

"Ah, Miss Kimball, we're sorry you failed to guess our mystery voice. The answer was, of course, Godzilla. But—"

"Is that you, Haskell?" I demanded.

"We're going to give you another chance. Even though you didn't win our first prize, ten free dance lessons with Mr. Smoot, we're going to give you the opportunity to win our second prize, which is twenty free dance lessons with Mr. Smoot. All you have to do is—"

"Haskell," I whispered viciously, "if you call me one more time, I'm going to steal your guinea pig and sell him to a research laboratory. LEAVE ME ALONE!"

I hung up, trembling. Had I really said that? Me, Dorrie Kimball, friend of animals, lover of nature? Had I really threatened to take my revenge on a harmless, fuzzy little creature?

What could make me say something like that?

Only Haskell, I thought grimly. No one else could make me that angry.

Except Conrad.

Later on Margaret's mother put out stuff for us to make hero sandwiches with, and we turned on the radio and danced. She said we'd have to wash the makeup off before we went to sleep.

"I thought we weren't going to sleep!" Eileen protested.

"What I mean is, if you get tired," Mrs. Cooper explained, "you'll want to wash before you settle down."

"Settle down?" Eileen repeated blankly.

But by midnight, Mrs. Cooper said we had to turn off the radio, because she and Mr. Cooper wanted to go to sleep, even if we didn't. And in fact, by then we had already lost a couple of people who had just laid down for a minute on their blankets to rest.

I finished up somebody's leftover sandwich and had another Coke. There had been another phone call for me, but I told Margaret to hang up on whoever it was. After she hung up, the phone had rung again, but she didn't answer it.

"I don't know," Serena was saying sleepily. "I think Warren is pretty stupid."

"Do you think he's stupid, Margaret?" Jackie asked, yawning.

"Well, he's not what you'd call *brilliant*," Margaret said.

"I think he's sort of cute," Jackie said.

"If you *didn't* think he was cute, I'd be surprised," Serena said sarcastically.

"Haskell is kind of nice," Margaret suggested, eyeing me.

"Haskell?" I snorted. "He's a monster. A living Frankenstein."

"Oh, he is not," Jackie protested. "You're prejudiced, that's all."

"I am not," I denied, "one bit prejudiced. I'm telling you, he's rotten; and his brother is exactly like him."

"Oh, garbage," Jackie said tiredly. She scrunched down into her sleeping bag.

"I *am* kind of tired," Serena yawned again, rolling herself up in her quilt.

"Are you?" asked Margaret, sounding disappointed. "I'm not a bit tired. Are you, Dorrie?"

"Nooo," I said dreamily, pulling my knees up and resting my head on my arm. "I'm not sleepy at all. In fact, I'm wide . . ."

EIGHT

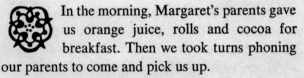In the morning, Margaret's parents gave us orange juice, rolls and cocoa for breakfast. Then we took turns phoning our parents to come and pick us up.

Before I got to use the phone, Mrs. Cooper came into the family room where we were doing a little straightening up.

"Dorrie? There's a person here who says he's supposed to drive you home." She had a suspicious look on her face, like she didn't believe it. When I followed her to the door, I understood why.

Dan stood uncertainly on the doorstep, his black hair long and shaggy, his plaid CPO jacket missing half a pocket and his ragged jeans almost covering the hiking boots he always wore, I could see that Mrs. Cooper thought he was more likely to be your friendly neighborhood mugger than my ride.

"Hi," he said weakly, from the other side of the glass door. "I'm supposed to take you home."

Behind me I could hear curious whispers and a few stifled giggles. Without turning around, I could picture fourteen girls, piled one on top of the other, peering out from behind the room divider which separated the living room and the dining room, trying to get a glimpse of Dan.

"Do you know this—person?" Margaret's mother asked in a strained voice.

"Oh, sure," I said, "that's Dan. He's my father's photographer. It's okay. My father must have asked him to pick me up."

"You're sure you don't want to call home?" she persisted.

"Oh, no," I assured her. "Dan is a trusted family friend." A fact which no doubt lowered her opinion of our family.

I went back to the family room to gather up my stuff and everyone bombarded me with questions.

"Who's that?" demanded Margaret.

"Is he your brother?"

"How old is he?"

"Is he in a rock group?"

"He's *cute*." That was Jackie, naturally.

"He's my father's photographer. For the *Leader*. He's twenty-two." I rolled up my blanket and collected my shopping bag.

They followed me through the kitchen like I was the Pied Piper of Hamelin and they were the rats.

"Thank you for inviting me," I said to Margaret. "It was a very good party."

"Thank you for coming," Margaret said automatically. She craned her neck to see past the other girls.

"Thank you, Mrs. Cooper," I remembered to say. "I had a very good time."

"You're welcome," she replied. She was still looking suspiciously at Dan. "Come again."

The girls followed me all the way to the front door, then stopped, bumping into each other behind me as I stepped outside.

"Goodby, Dorrie! Goodby, Dorrie!" They waved as if I were leaving for a round-the-world trip and wouldn't be back for three years.

Their chorus followed me down the steps.

"See you Monday!" they persisted. I could still hear them as I climbed into Dan's ten-year-old Volkswagen.

"Have a good time?" Dan asked as he coaxed the car into starting.

"Yeah. It was nice." I waved back at everyone

as we pulled away from the curb. "How come you're here?"

"Your father and I are going to do some work this morning," he explained. "This was right on the way to your house; I told him I'd pick you up. Let him sleep five minutes longer."

"You're going to work on Sunday?"

"Yeah, well that was the only time I had," he said. "He didn't like the idea too much either. I tried to call you last night to tell you, but someone hung up on me, then no one answered."

"Ohh—that was the one time I told Margaret to hang up."

I explained about the phone calls, and while I told Dan about them, I started getting angry all over again.

"They must like you," Dan said casually.

"Like me? They hate me!"

"Wrong. If they hated you, they wouldn't call you."

"Don't be silly. They called to bother me."

"But they wouldn't bother bothering you if they didn't like you," he insisted.

"That doesn't make sense," I retorted.

"Okay, okay, don't get mad. I could be wrong."

"Of course you're wrong. Boy, are you ever wrong!"

We drove up to the house.

"Thanks for the ride," I said coldly.

"No trouble," he shrugged.

Why, I wondered, stomping up to the door, why was I so angry?

After the pajama party the weeks ran together like a blur. The only thing I could think about was our Book Week newspaper. I would be in the middle of watching television and an idea would come to me. Or I'd be brushing my teeth and all of a sudden I would think, "Piper's Son, Tom, Steals Pig. Escapes Police Dragnet."

There didn't seem to be enough time to work on our project during school, so I began to call committee meetings for after school at my house.

The first one we had, Haskell came late.

"I asked you to come at four," I said irritably, when he wandered in at four-thirty.

"Got held up in traffic," he shrugged.

But after that, he was usually on time. Most surprising of all, he began to work almost as hard as the rest of us on the articles and headlines.

A couple of times my father sat in on our meetings, and explained to us about counting paragraph inches and leaving enough space for pictures, and making headlines fit the columns and setting up a dummy page.

"I didn't realize," Serena said at one of these meetings, "how much work this was going to be."

"Neither did I," I admitted.

Charles and I began typing up the stories. Time was running out and even as we began to type up our final copies for the printer, we kept thinking of new ideas for articles.

TOM SAWYER HOLDS PAINT-IN YOUNGSTERS FLOCK TO TAKE PART IN STREET BEAUTIFICATION PROJECT

Serena drew picture after picture, till she had one for almost every story we'd written. Then we made up captions for them: "Little Women who want to do their bit for the soldiers. Meg, Jo, Beth and Amy knit stockings for the Union cause."

The Wednesday before Book Week we met at my house and made our final choices of articles and pictures. We did a rough layout, as my father had explained, to get an idea of where we'd put everything, and how the paper would look when it was finished.

On Thursday morning, my father took all our material to the office with him. The printers were going to set up the galleys, and he would bring the proofs home in the afternoon.

That day the committee had its final meeting. We had to proofread everything to check for mistakes and correct the few we found. Then we had to cut stories out of the long sheets of paper that were the galley proofs and paste them onto a dummy sheet the same size as our newspaper.

My mother made franks and beans for everyone so no one would have to go home for dinner. We didn't finish the paper until seven-thirty.

When it was finally done, my father checked it over one last time while we slumped, exhausted, on the living room floor.

"This is a fine job," he announced at last.

"Thank goodness!" Serena sighed with relief.

Haskell gave a weak cheer, and slapped hands with Charles.

"Now how many copies should I make up?" my father asked.

"I never thought of that," I realized. "I guess one for everybody in the class, and an extra one for Mrs. O'Neill."

"You know, once the type is set it's as easy to make a hundred as it is to make twenty-five," he said.

"Then why don't we make enough for the whole school?" Serena suggested eagerly. "Mrs. O'Neill wants to display the projects and have the other classes come in and see them. She said we would do things the whole school could enjoy—"

"So you'll need about a thousand?"

"Will that be too expensive?" I worried.

"No, it's all right," he assured me. "With the free advertising you gave me, it's worth it."

On the front page in a little box, we had set up a plug for my father's paper. It read: "The *Book Week Leader* is grateful to the *Brockton Center Leader* for printing this special edition. For news of the *real* world, read the *Leader* every Thursday."

At first my father hadn't wanted to put it in, being against nepotism and everything. But the committee insisted. We said if he made us leave it out, it would be censorship. If there's one thing my father hates more than nepotism, it's censorship; so he finally agreed to let us do it.

I couldn't wait for school to be over on Friday. My father was going to bring the finished paper home with him, and I was a nervous wreck all day, wondering how it would turn out.

At lunch Margaret told us excitedly about her birthday. It was two weeks away, and she was going to celebrate it with her closest friends.

"My parents are going to take us to the city, and we'll go out to dinner, and then we're going to the Ice Capades. At *night!*" she emphasized, looking around to see our reactions.

"Oh, Margaret," Jackie cried, "that's fantastic!"

"Who are you inviting?" asked Serena.

"Oh, I don't know," Margaret said carelessly. "I haven't really decided yet."

"Come on, Margaret!" Jackie pleaded. "Don't be like that."

"Don't be such a dummy!" laughed Margaret. "You're invited. *Naturally*."

"Am I invited?" Serena asked uncertainly.

"Of course you are. And you too, Dorrie."

"Oh!" I really hadn't expected to be. Especially after the pajama party and all those telephone calls.

"Thanks," I said. "It sounds great." It really did, too. But until the *Book Week Leader* was safely printed and handed out to everyone, I couldn't really work up too much excitement for anything else.

My father came home just before dinner and I flung myself at him when he was barely over the threshold.

"Let me see it! Did it come out okay? *How does it look?*"

"Here," he said, handing me a bunch of papers. "See for yourself. I think it came out beautifully."

My mother came up behind me and reached for a copy. "I've been waiting all day for this. Oh, Dorrie! It's beautiful!" She sat down on the couch and began to read it. She turned the pages eagerly. Every once in a while she smiled or laughed, and pointed out something she especially liked to my father.

It *was* beautiful. It looked just like the *Leader,* but it had only four pages. *Book Week Leader* was in the same kind of type my father uses for *Brockton Center Leader* on the top of the front page. Serena's pictures had come out perfectly.

I smiled as I re-read the stories and headlines that I already knew practically by heart.

R. CRUSOE LOST AT SEA

TORNADO RIPS HOUSE FROM KANSAS FARM
Girl, Dog and House Vanish During Killer Storm

QUICK-THINKING YOUNGSTER PLUGS DIKE
Saves Holland from Flood Disaster

"Oh, it's gorgeous, gorgeous!" I cried. "Isn't it? Oh, it's just the way I pictured it. No, it's *better!*"

The doorbell rang.

"Hi," said Haskell as I opened the door.

"What do you want?"

"I saw your father come home. Is the paper done?"

I thrust it at him. "Here. I think it's beautiful."

"Hey." He turned it over and looked through it. "Hey, that's all right."

"It's better than all right," I said coldly.

"Can I take it home with me?" he asked. "I want to show it to my mother. And Conrad."

I didn't know you cared that much, I said to myself.

"Sure, take it," I told him indifferently.

"We have plenty," said my father. He sounded as if he were picking out his words very carefully. "If you want an extra copy to send your dad . . ."

"Nah," Haskell mumbled, looking uncomfortable. "He wouldn't be interested."

I watched him trudge down the steps. I slowly closed the front door.

"Isn't that a shame?" my mother said. "Those poor boys."

I was about to say something nasty when suddenly I felt an emptiness in my stomach. I looked at my parents. For some strange reason, I couldn't think up one rotten remark to make about Haskell or Conrad.

That's odd, I thought, puzzled. I certainly couldn't have run out of nasty things to say about them all of a sudden like this.

Oh well, it's late, I realized. I patted my empty-feeling stomach. I'm probably just hungry.

nine

When I woke up Monday morning it was snowing. And my throat hurt. I swallowed a couple of times and it still hurt.

"Ah," I said softly, testing my voice. "Helloo, helloo." Well, my voice was still there.

I practiced saying, "I feel fine," while I got dressed, just in case my parents sensed something. Today was not the day to be sick. Today was the day to hand out the *Book Week Leader*. I could be sick tomorrow, maybe. Not today.

At breakfast no one said a word about my health. They were watching the snow and listening to the weather reports on the radio.

Dan came by at a quarter of nine. He was

going to help haul the cartons of newspapers from the trunk and the back seat of our car into school.

Just as we were ready to leave, my father spotted Haskell and Conrad coming out of their house.

"Come on with us!" he shouted, before I could stop him.

They trotted toward our car like twin joggers, and climbed into the back seat.

"Thanks," they said together.

"Don't thank me," my father said, as Dan and I squeezed into the front seat. "I have an ulterior motive. You can help us get these papers in. We've got six cartons of them."

My father double-parked in front of the main entrance to the school and we each carried in a carton. They weighed about a ton apiece, and we practically staggered up the steps and inside.

Charles and Serena were already there, waiting for us.

Serena grabbed a paper from one of the cartons. "Oh, it looks great!" she exclaimed, holding it a little away from herself like she was admiring a painting.

"You can look at it later," Charles said, hoisting a pile of papers up to the Lost and Found table. "Let's get set up before the kids start coming in. We have two other entrances to cover."

Serena had made three posters which read:

BOOK WEEK LEADER FREE! TAKE ONE! She'd already taped one to the Lost and Found table, pushing aside the stray gloves, hats, scarves and gym shirts so we'd have a place to put the papers. The other two posters were for the other doors to the school, where she and Charles were going to hand out papers to the kids who came in that way.

"Before you go," my father said to Charles and Serena, "let's have Dan take a picture of the committee in front of the poster. We'll have copies made up for all of you; then you'll always have something to remind you of how hard you worked on this."

"Oh, I'll never forget *that,*" Serena groaned.

Haskell, Serena, Charles and I grouped ourselves behind the table and held up a copy of the *Book Week Leader.*

"Don't all stare at the camera," my father advised. "Dorrie, open the paper and everybody pretend to be reading it."

So I did, holding it up so the front page would show in the picture.

"Now look at the paper, don't look at Dan."

"Got it!" Dan said as the flashbulb blazed.

"Okay," my father said. "We've got to get to a town board meeting now. I'll have those pictures made up for you in a couple of days."

"So long," I said, patting his arm. "Thanks a lot, Dad."

"It was fun," he said. "Sort of. Good luck!"

Now we really had to rush. Charles and Serena each took a carton of papers and a poster and staggered off to set themselves up at the other doors. Kids were already starting to come in the main entrance.

Conrad grabbed a pile of papers.

"Wuxtry wuxtry, read all about it!" he chanted. "Robinson Crusoe lost at sea!" He thrust a paper at everyone who passed.

"What's this?"

"Your free Book Week newspaper."

"Hey, this is neat. Who did it?"

"Wuxtry wuxtry!"

The crush had started. Suddenly we were mobbed. Everyone was snatching copies. Conrad, who was still shouting, was surrounded. I had to reach over people's heads and arms to hand papers to the kids who couldn't get to the table. Haskell was using both hands to distribute copies, and looked a little frazzled.

A major traffic jam was building up between the main door and our table. Kids were stopping to examine the papers, and the kids behind them were finding it impossible to move down the hall.

Conrad came to get another pile of papers.

"Will you stop shouting wuxtry!" I said irritably. I felt like I was in the midst of an angry mob. Hands groped toward me for papers. "It sounds stupid!"

"All the newsboys say 'wuxtry,'" Conrad retorted.

"I never heard one say it."

"Well they do," Conrad insisted. "All the time in the movies."

"This isn't the movies," I reminded him. "Ow! Hey, leave my fingers on my hand, please. There's enough for everyone."

My head was beginning to hurt and my throat was still sore. I felt hot and the crowd was beginning to seem more like a prison riot than a bunch of kids.

But the paper was obviously a huge success. I could hear people reading headlines out loud to each other. They moved slowly away from the table, papers held up in front of them, not looking where they were going because they were so absorbed in the *Book Week Leader*.

"Contrary Mary Plants People. Green Thumb Raises Pretty Maids All in Row. Botanists Mystified. Scientists Astounded."

"Hood Eludes Sheriff Again. Bandit Leader and Merry Men Gang Still at Large."

"What in the world is this?"

I looked up into the face of Mrs. Grant, the principal.

"This is our Book Week project," I explained. "We're giving everyone a copy of our *Book Week Leader*."

"You should have asked permission to distribute anything in this area," she frowned. "You're creating quite a disturbance."

"I'm sorry," I said weakly. "I didn't think—"

She picked up a paper and scanned it. "This is

very good," she smiled. "You must have put a lot of hard work into it."

"We did," I nodded.

"Well, next time ask me before you start handing out something. We could distribute it to each class from the office. This is really impossible."

"Okay," I promised.

She pushed her way through the crowd of people in front of the desk. She was still holding on to the paper she'd picked up.

"All right, people, let's keep it moving! Get your papers and then go right to your rooms. Come on!"

Finally the crowd thinned out till there were no more people in the corridor. Haskell, Conrad and I looked at each other and breathed a huge sigh of relief.

"Thank goodness that's over," I croaked.

We gathered up the remaining papers and our cartons, took our poster off the table, and trudged down the hall toward the sixth-grade classrooms.

Haskell and I got to our room as the pledge of allegiance was being recited, so we waited outside the door until everyone sat down.

"You're late," Mrs. O'Neill observed sternly as we opened the door.

"Happy Book Week!" Haskell said. He handed her a *Leader*.

Everyone in the class had a copy on their desk.

"We were handing them out," I explained. Charles and Serena burst into the room, red-faced and breathless.

"It was our committee project."

"We were handing them out too," Serena panted, trying to catch her breath.

But Mrs. O'Neill didn't even seem to be listening. She was reading the *Book Week Leader* as if she couldn't take her eyes off it.

"All right," she said absently. "Take your seats."

"Your attention please." Mrs. Grant's voice came over the PA system.

"I hope you will all be sure to take time today to read the *Book Week Leader*. This special newspaper was prepared in honor of Children's Book Week by four students in Mrs. O'Neill's class. I want to congratulate Dorrie Kimball, and her committee, Serena Blood, Charles Abbot and Haskell Conger—"

How did she know our names, I wondered. Then I realized we had listed the newspaper committee under "Staff" in a box on the back page.

"—for a very entertaining and informative newspaper."

Even though my throat was on fire and my head throbbed, I had never felt better in my life. I sat up very straight in my seat and exchanged big smiles with Serena, who looked as proud as I did.

Haskell was grinning from ear to ear. He held up two fingers in the victory sign. I smiled back at him. Charles was leaning back in his chair, hands clasped over his stomach. He looked as satisfied as a cat who's just finished off a dish of mouse à la mode.

"Our project was just a dumb old diorama," Jackie remarked glumly.

We spent most of the morning setting up our projects around the room. Each of the committee chairmen described their projects and how they were done. I don't even remember what I said, because by that time I really felt awful, and I was sure I had a fever of about 109°.

But I didn't want to go down to the nurse's office and be sent home. Not today. Even if I was on the verge of pneumonia, I was enjoying myself more than I ever had in school. I didn't want to miss one minute of this day.

While I don't remember what I said about our project, I remember very well what Mrs. O'Neill said.

"This is a marvelous, original idea. You did a beautiful job. I just don't see how you could have made it any better."

And in the afternoon, although I still felt sick, I enjoyed hearing the kids in the other classes, whom Mrs. O'Neill had invited to see our projects, exclaim, "Oh there's the paper!" It had been pasted up on the outside of the classroom door.

But by three o'clock I was glad that it was time to go home. I was too tired to think straight. I kept swallowing, even though it hurt to swallow, because my mouth was so dry that images of hot sands and cactus kept coming into my mind.

It was still snowing. I hurried past the snowball throwers and trudged toward home. The snow was sticking, and had already covered the lawns and sidewalks, tops of houses, trees and fences. Everything looked beautiful, and the flakes blowing against my face cooled me off. I scooped a little snow off a bush and popped it into my mouth. It was delicious.

I passed Haskell and Conrad's house, my face turned up to the sky, my mouth open to catch the snowflakes.

"Aiiee—yah!" came a hideous scream.

I whirled around, and two snowballs smashed against my chest.

Haskell and Conrad popped up from behind their hedge.

"GOTCHA!"

They popped down again, out of sight.

"Oh yeah?" I scooped up a handful of snow.

One of them stood up again, his arm raised.

"HA!" I shrieked, and hurled my snowball at

him. "Gotcha!" I crowed as he dropped out of sight.

"Right between the eyes," I chuckled evilly.

The other one popped up. This is like ducks in a shooting gallery, I thought frantically. I grabbed another handful of snow and packed it firmly.

Not fast enough.

"POW!" he yelled, letting it fly.

I ducked. "Pow yourself! You missed, stupid!"

Up popped a twin.

"ZAP!" I croaked, hurling my snowball. This was not doing my throat one bit of good.

"You missed too!" he taunted, from behind the hedge.

This is terrible, I told myself suddenly. There were two of them and one of me, and they were behind a fortress, practically, while I was a perfect, out-in-the-open target.

I had to get to them, behind that hedge.

I raced around the back of my house, across my yard and over their fence. I could see them squatting next to the hedge, busily piling up a supply of snowballs. Creeping silently along the side of their house, I spotted their milk delivery box by the side door. It was open, and full of snow.

I snatched it up and continued my stealthy approach.

One of them raised himself up to peer over the hedge.

"She's not there."

I charged. "HERE I AM!" I screeched, raising the milk box to hurl the snow inside right into their faces.

The element of surprise is always a powerful advantage, but one person with a milk box full of snow against two people with a stockpile of about two hundred snowballs (or maybe it just seemed like two hundred) doesn't have much of an advantage—surprise or no surprise.

And besides, I had yelled, "Here I am," too soon and from too far away.

A torrent of snowballs pelted me. The air was thick with "Gotchas!" I held the milk box in front of my face as a shield, and charged forward.

Of course, I couldn't see where I was going. I ran straight into the pile of snowballs, tripped over someone's legs, and plopped down.

"This is awfully cold," I murmured, with what little was left of my voice.

"That's because you're sitting on our ammunition," Haskell pointed out.

Suddenly I was so weak and tired, I couldn't get up.

I scooped out a handful of snow from the milk box, which was now on my lap, and tossed it half-heartedly at the nearest face.

"Gotcha," I whimpered hoarsely.

I scooped out another handful of snow. I looked

at it, puzzled. What did I want to do with it? I couldn't remember.

"I think," I announced, "it's time for me to go home now."

I continued to sit among the squashed snowballs.

"Are you all right?" Conrad asked curiously.

"No," I replied, "I am probably not all right at all. In fact, I may be dying. I may even be delirious. Do you think I'm delirious?"

"No more than usual."

"Is that your milk box?" I asked suddenly.

"Come on," said Haskell. He stood up and yanked me to my feet. "You better go home now."

"Of course," I said reasonably. "That's what I said."

I staggered out from behind the hedge and weaved across my white front lawn to our door.

I rang the bell.

"Dorrie!" my mother shrieked. "What happened to you?"

"I don't feel so good."

"You're soaking wet!" she cried.

"Yes," I nodded. "Maybe that's why."

"Did you fall in the snow? What happened?"

"I lost," I sighed sorrowfully.

ten

"I'm dying," I groaned as my mother tried to get me out of bed the next morning.

"I know you feel terrible," she said sympathetically. "That's why we're going to the doctor."

"Doesn't the doctor know I'm dying?" I asked weakly. "Why doesn't he come here?"

"He says it won't hurt to bring you to his office."

"Sure," I croaked. "Won't hurt *him*."

I crawled out of bed reluctantly, and let my mother help me get dressed.

I couldn't remember getting *into* bed. I couldn't remember last night. In fact, I couldn't remember anything after the snowball fight.

"What day is it?"

"Tuesday," she said, surprised.

"What happened to the rest of Monday?" I wondered.

"You've been sleeping, on and off, since early yesterday evening."

"My mind," I declared somberly, "is a total blank."

It had stopped snowing, but our street hadn't been plowed yet because we aren't a main road. My mother had to drive very slowly till we got to Tebbits Boulevard.

We had had six inches of snow, she told me, and it had stopped last night, while I was asleep. Dan had taken my father to work so that she could have the car to drive me to the doctor. She was supposed to call my father at the office the minute we got home.

The doctor's waiting room was full of people. They were coughing, sneezing, holding their stomachs or just sitting weakly on plastic chairs, gazing blankly into space.

"This place is full of sick people," I hissed.

"What did you expect?"

"I might catch something else," I scowled, "and get even sicker."

"I don't see how you could be much sicker," my mother said, patting my hand gently.

We waited so long to see the doctor, that I was

nearly asleep in my chair when we were finally called in.

My ears, nose and throat were poked and peered into. My back and chest were listened to with a cold stethoscope. My temperature was taken.

"How do you feel?" the doctor asked.

I gazed at him blankly. How did he think I felt? Couldn't he see that I was dying?

"Rotten," I replied hoarsely.

"Fine, fine," he muttered.

"What is it, Doctor?" asked my mother anxiously.

"Oh, it's going around."

What's going around? I wondered.

"But what is it?" she persisted.

"I've seen a lot of it in the past few days," he replied.

A lot of what, I asked silently.

"Is it serious?" my mother asked nervously.

Is *what* serious?

"No, no, she'll just feel pretty bad for a couple of days."

"Can you give her something for it?"

"No, there's nothing to give. It goes by itself."

"What have I got?" I demanded finally.

"What everybody else has got," he said cheerfully. "Now just open your mouth again, and we'll take a throat culture. We want to be absolutely certain it isn't a strep infection."

He scraped the back of my throat with something and I thought I was going to choke.

"Fine, fine," he murmured.

"What should we do for her?" my mother asked.

"Oh, she'll probably want to rest, mostly. And she won't feel like eating much. Give her plenty to drink, though. Aspirin. And watch her temperature. I'm pretty sure it isn't strep, but if it is, my office will call you tomorrow and I'll prescribe penicillin."

"Couldn't you give her penicillin now?" asked my mother.

"Oh, no, only if the throat culture is positive. Penicillin doesn't have any effect on a virus."

A virus! I thought triumphantly. That's what I've got. A plain old virus. My mother is too smart for you, Doctor, I gloated inwardly. You tried to keep it from us, but she wormed it out of you.

"Nice going, Mom," I congratulated her.

The doctor said I could go back to school when my temperature had been normal for two days. He said I'd probably have to be home for a week.

When we got back to the house, my mother sent me to bed, and went to call my father.

I fell asleep almost instantly.

My mother put the portable television in my

room and I stayed in bed, even for meals. I didn't feel very hungry, but she kept bringing me juice and soda and soup.

The next day I felt a little better. My fever had gone down a degree and my throat wasn't so sore.

"There's a letter for you," she said, bringing it into my room with a glass of ginger ale.

It was a small envelope, and it wasn't from Marlene. It must be an invitation to Margaret's birthday, I thought. I tore it open.

It wasn't an invitation to anything. It was a birth announcement.

On the front of the card there was a picture of a little baby. Printed over his head was, "It's a boy!" Under the picture someone had added, in ball point pen: "And a girl and another boy and another girl. Probably."

What in the world?

Inside the card had been filled out: *Parents:* Little Caesar and Friend *Weight: ? Length:* 3 inches *Date:* Nov. 10 *Names:* (The "s" had been added to "Name" with a pen) Spanky, Hopalong, Ruby and Racquel.

"Will you look at that!" I giggled. "Little Caesar had babies!"

My mother examined the card and began to laugh. "A birth announcement for a guinea pig?"

"Isn't that funny?" I grinned.

"Yes," she said slowly. Her eyes scanned my

face as if she were trying to look into my mind. "It *is* funny, isn't it?"

Serena called me that afternoon.

"Are you sick?" she asked.

"Yeah. I've got a virus."

"Oh, that's too bad. We had more classes in today to look at the projects. Mrs. O'Neill said that a lot of teachers were asking for copies of the paper. You left some of the extras in school, so I gave her a bunch. Was that okay?"

"Sure," I said, flattered.

"Some of the teachers want to use our idea themselves. You know, have the kids do newspaper stories on the books they're reading and then make a class newspaper out of it."

"Did they say that?" I asked.

"Yeah, they did. They were really excited about the idea. But they'll only mimeograph theirs. Nobody's will be as good as ours," Serena said proudly.

I was sure of that.

I had barely gotten off the phone with Serena when it rang again. This time it was Margaret.

"Dorrie? How come you weren't in school?"

I told her.

"Oh, no," she moaned. "I hope you get better in time for my birthday."

"Sure," I said. "This only lasts a couple of days."

"Oh, good." She sounded relieved. "Well, listen, I'd come over and visit you—"

"That would be great!" I said. "I'm getting kind of bored with quiz shows and soap operas."

"—except that I might catch your virus," she went on smoothly, "and I don't want to be sick for my birthday."

"No," I agreed glumly. "That would be terrible."

"Well, so long," she said. "You get better real fast."

"I'll try," I said weakly, hoping to make her feel a little guilty.

"We wouldn't want you to miss the big night!" She didn't sound the least bit guilty.

"Me neither," I said. " 'Bye."

" 'Bye."

I dropped the phone back on the hook. I walked slowly to my room and got into bed again.

Marlene, I thought resentfully, would have been here the minute she got home from school. She wouldn't have worried about a dumb old germ—even if she were on her way to swim in the Olympics, she would have come to see me anyway.

Oh, well, I sighed. Margaret is Margaret. She

can't be expected to be Marlene; not when she's so—so—*Margaret.*

That's very intelligent, Dorrie, I told myself. That makes a lot of sense. This virus is probably affecting your brain. Sure it is. You're talking to yourself. There you go again, one half of you talking to the other half.

"I'm not well," I whispered gravely.

The doorbell rang. Sherman barked hysterically.

"Who is it?" I yelled, and clutched my throat.

"Don't scream," my mother called back. "You'll hurt your throat. It's Haskell and Conrad."

Haskell and Conrad?

I heard their voices downstairs. Sherman whined anxiously.

"They say," my mother called, "that they're immune to every disease known to man. Can they come up?"

"Okay," I said hoarsely. I was desperate for the sight of a human face. (My mother and father don't count.) Even subhuman, I added automatically. But I didn't feel that sudden flash of anger that I was so used to whenever the twins were mentioned. How strange, I thought.

"Howdy, ma'am," one of them said as they came into my room. Sherman trotted in behind them, sniffing at their legs.

"Hi, Conrad."

"We're powerful sorry you're ailin'," said Haskell. He was carrying something large and square, wrapped in brown paper.

"We feel a mite guilty," said Conrad, trying to look remorseful by staring down at his feet.

"You feel guilty?" I thought of Margaret.

"For ambushin' you in the snow and bringin' on sickness and sufferin'."

"You didn't make me sick," I said. "I was sick when I went to school. I just didn't tell anyone."

They looked at each other for a second. They seemed almost relieved, like they had really been feeling bad about the whole thing.

"Oh, boy, that's good!" Haskell exclaimed in his normal voice. "I mean, not that you're sick—"

"Yeah, I know," I reassured him. "Hey, what's that package?"

He put the big square thing down on the floor and started ripping the paper off.

"It's for you," he said. "Part of a present."

It was a cage, built out of wood and window screening. Sherman walked carefully around it, sniffing from every angle.

"The other part is too young to leave her mother yet."

"Oh! You mean I can have one of Little Caesar's babies?"

"With our compliments," Haskell said, bowing low.

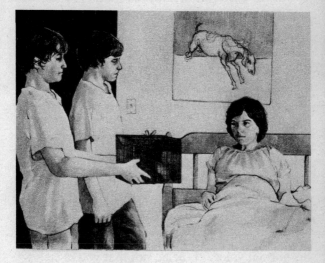

"Just keep *him* away from it," warned Conrad, "and let them get used to each other gradually."

"Then Little Caesar didn't have a nervous breakdown?" I asked.

"No," said Conrad, "but we didn't realize she was pregnant until she suddenly got real fat, and then we took her to the vet again, and he told us that must be why she was acting so funny."

"Why didn't you tell me?" I demanded. "Why did you let me go on thinking it was Sherman's fault that she was like that?"

"You didn't ask us," Haskell said mildly. "We didn't know you were interested."

116

"Oh," I said softly. What else could I say? It was true.

"She must have been pregnant when we got her," Conrad was saying. "But we didn't even know she was female. We just never thought to ask."

"Yeah," I grinned sheepishly. "There's a lot of that going around."

All of a sudden the twins didn't seem like my enemies. They're not so terrible, I thought. They're really not so terrible at all.

I smiled happily. Haskell smiled back.

"Well, listen," he said, "I hope you feel better soon. And we'll bring Racquel over in a week or two."

"Thanks," I said. "I can't wait to see her."

"And if she turns out to be a boy," added Conrad, "you can call her Rocky."

"But—how will I know?" I asked uncertainly.

"Beats me," Conrad shrugged.

eleven

My father came home very late that evening. He always does on Wednesdays, since the *Leader* comes out on Thursdays and they have to finish everything up.

"How are you feeling?" he asked, coming into my room with my mother.

"A little better," I said.

"Not at death's door any more?"

"No," I grinned. "Hey, you know I'm going to get a guinea pig?"

"Really? How's that?"

"Hal," my mother said, "will you please—"

"Little Caesar had babies. Did you see the card Haskell and Conrad sent me?" I scrambled around

119

my messy bed looking for the birth announcement.

"HAL," my mother repeated loudly.

I looked up, surprised by the tone of her voice.

"What's the matter?" I asked.

"Oh, your mother's very worked up about something she saw in the paper," he grinned.

"In what paper? The *Leader?*" There's usually only local news in my father's paper, and I can never find anything in it to get worked up about. Maybe they were raising town taxes, or building a swamp across the street from our house.

"What is it?" I asked curiously.

"Oh, nothing," he said carelessly. He handed me the paper, opened to an inside page. "Just that."

The headline and picture leaped out at me from the page.

STUDENTS PUBLISH SPECIAL ISSUE OF LEADER
Book Week Project Surprises Parkview School

And next to the story, the picture Dan had taken of us, holding up the *Book Week Leader,* with Charles, Serena and Haskell reading it over my shoulder.

I just sat there with my mouth open, unable to say a word. I touched the picture with my fingertips, trying to convince myself that it was real.

"Dorrie Kimball," it said under the picture, "with her committee, Serena Blood, Charles Abbot and Haskell Conger, reading the hot-off-the-presses *Book Week Leader*."

"You put my picture in the paper," I said at last. "You really put my picture in the paper."

"Read the story," my mother urged. "See what Mrs. O'Neill said."

My eyes raced down the column. I couldn't even concentrate on what I was reading, I was so dazed. Mrs. O'Neill had said something about not believing it could be done by students our age, and wondering how we ever managed to accomplish such a major undertaking.

"I can't believe it," I breathed. "I just—I mean, nepotism and all—"

"This isn't nepotism," my father objected, grinning broadly. "You did something newsworthy. I told you before, all you had to do to get your picture in the paper was—"

"OHH!" I shrieked, leaping up onto my bed and flinging the paper into the air. "I'm in the *paper!* I'm famous!"

I hurled myself at my parents, hugging both of them so hard, I nearly knocked their heads together.

"Dorrie!" they gasped, hugging me back. *"Please!"*